To my great friend Line.
L.P.

Leon the Raccoon

Explores the Arctic

by Lucie Papineau

Illustrations by Tommy Doyle

AUZOU

Leon and his friend Gaspard
watch the sun rise over the
sleeping city.
"Look," Leon says, pointing
at the sky, "Snow geese!"

"They're flying north to their summer home in the Arctic.
I wish we could follow them..." Leon whispers.

"My mom is flying to the Arctic to deliver supplies to a school there for Spring term. She's a pilot! Maybe we can go with her," exclaims Gaspard.

"Oh, please? I want to go! I want to go!" Leon begs.
"Well, I don't see why not," replies Mama Fox. "But you
must promise to behave… both of you!"
"Oh, we will!" the young explorers shout.

Leon and Gaspard fasten their seat belts, and put on their goggles. Their eyes open wide as the small plane speeds down the runway, then climbs high into the sky. "Here's to new adventures," Leon crows.

"Look at those boats," Leon yells to his friend. "They look like toys. And the trees… they look like broccoli!"

"There's the tree line," says Mama Fox, pointing to where the last tree tops can be seen.

"Trees can't grow in the frozen tundra," Gaspard explains to his friend.

"We're not far
from the village,"
their pilot announces.

Just then, the engine starts making a funny, coughing noise and sways from left to right. Mama Fox must make an emergency landing!

Whew! Landing the small plane on the ice wasn't too difficult, but now what? The plane can't fly with a broken engine!
Mama Fox is worried. How will she get the books, pencils and notebooks to the children in time for the start of school?

On the other hand, Leon and Gaspard are thrilled. They are surrounded by water and ice, lost on a small island in the middle of nowhere... just like real explorers!

Leon spots a gigantic polar bear swimming in the icy water. "Hey, Mr. Big Bear," calls the little raccoon who isn't the least bit afraid. "Can you help us?"
"Indeed," answers the friendly giant.

No sooner said than done, Mama Fox and the two boys load the crate of supplies on the polar bear's back and climb aboard.

Leon and Gaspard smile and wave as they pass some sleepy walruses.

Finally, they reach land, but how will they find their way in this immense and lonely place?

Leon, always curious, spots a majestic snowy owl in the sky. "Hello, Mrs. Bird," he calls out. "Can you help us?"
"I'd be happy to," the owl responds, landing silently.

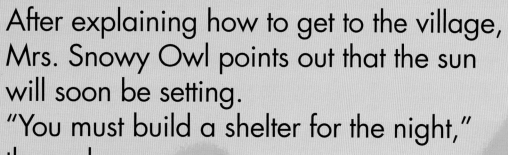

After explaining how to get to the village,
Mrs. Snowy Owl points out that the sun
will soon be setting.
"You must build a shelter for the night,"
the owl warns.

Mama Fox, Gaspard, and Leon quickly construct an igloo.
"This is fun!" the boys giggle. "It's like building with giant blocks!"

Before they fall asleep, the friends see an Arctic spectacle: the Aurora Borealis.

"Wow!" says Leon. "The Northern Lights! I never dreamed they would be so beautiful!"

The next morning, a light snow falls from the cloud-covered sky. Worried, Mama Fox scans the horizon… but who does she see? Why, it's the Arctic hares to the rescue! News travels fast here.

One, two, three…HOP! The hares take off across the snow while Leon and Gaspard laugh in their improvised sled.

It isn't long before they spot the village in the distance. The tiny town is nestled in a bay; the Arctic Ocean is its garden.

Thanks to the courage of Mama Fox and her young co-pilots, the village school can finally re-open its doors. The whole town turns out to celebrate!

All their new friends are here, even the walruses have come
now that they managed to fix Mama Fox's plane!
Suddenly, Leon hears honking. What is that? he wonders,
thinking it sounds familiar.

Everyone looks up as the flock of snow geese
flies overhead. The warm spring sun has
begun to melt the snow, and the first flowers
are about to bloom. What an amazing place
to spend the summer!

"I knew we would see them again," whispers
Leon as dreams of his next adventure dance
in his head...

ISBN: 978-2-7338-5045-9

Senior Editor: Laura Levy
Editor: Juliette Féquant
Assistant Editor: Adrienne Heymans
Art Director: Alice Nominé
Layout: Eloïse Jensen, Alice Vignaux
Production Manager: Jean-Christophe Collett
Production Controller: Virginie Champeaud
Project Management for the present edition: Ariane Laine-Forrest
Written by Lucie Papineau
Illustrations by Tommy Doyle
English translation by MaryChris Bradley

First published in French as Les aventures de Léon le raton dans le grand Nord
Copyright © 2017, Éditions Auzou
24 -32 rue des Amandiers 75020 Paris, France.

Printed in China